Norman Gale

Orchard Songs

I DEDICATE

THESE COUNTRY AIRS

TO THOSE FRIENDS OF MINE

ALFRED HAYES AND

RICHARD LE GALLIENNE

AS AN ATTEMPTED PROOF OF

FRIENDSHIP EQUAL TO

THEIR OWN

a 2

Norman Gale

Orchard Songs

ISBN/EAN: 9783744769730

Printed in Europe, USA, Canada, Australia, Japan

Cover: Foto ©Andreas Hilbeck / pixelio.de

More available books at **www.hansebooks.com**

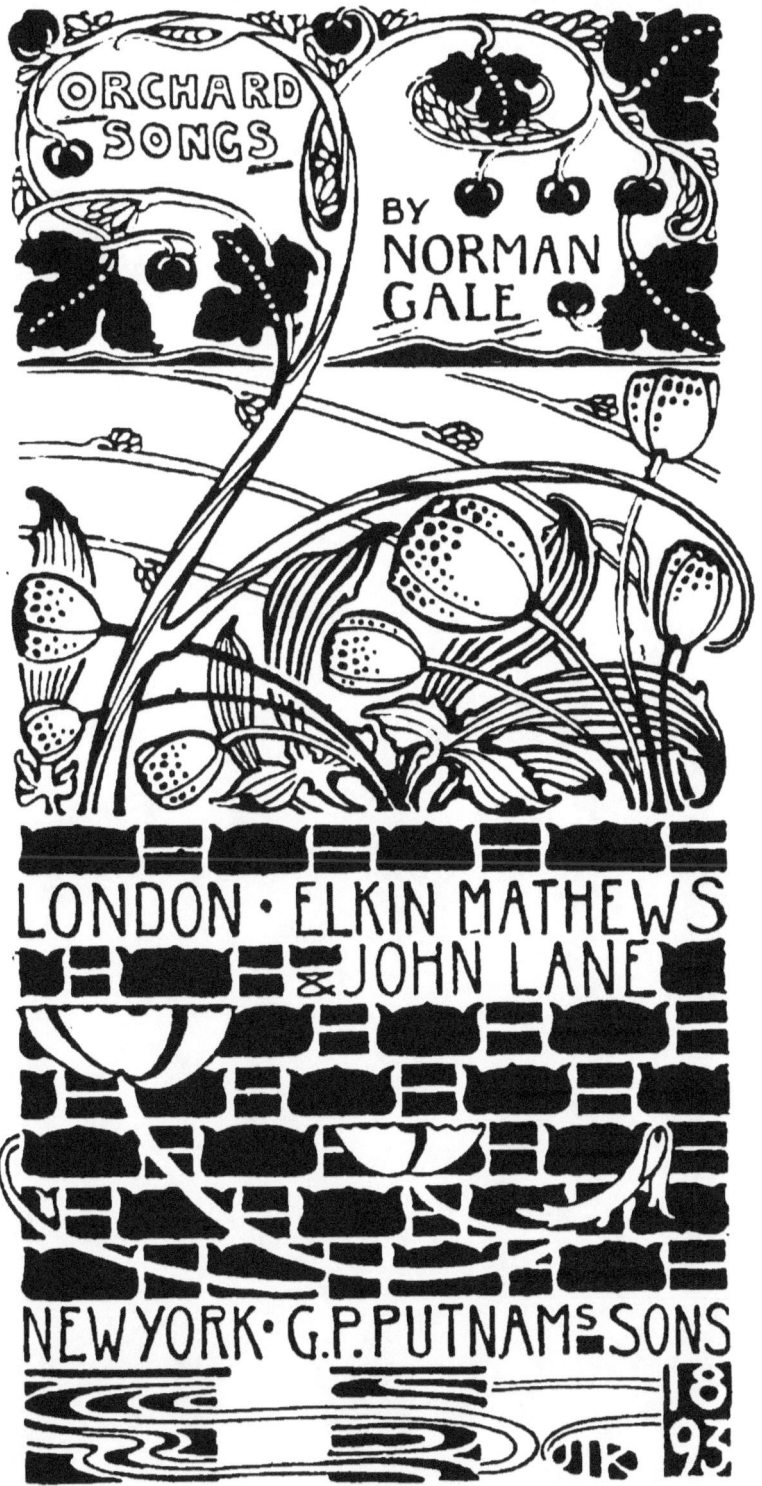

ORCHARD SONGS

BY NORMAN GALE

LONDON · ELKIN MATHEWS & JOHN LANE

NEW YORK · G.P. PUTNAMS SONS

1893

For permission to reprint, my thanks are heartily due to the Editors of 'The Christian World,' the 'Pall Mall Magazine,' the 'Literary World,' the 'English Illustrated Magazine,' and 'The Woman at Home.'

CONTENTS

CONTENTS

x

CONTENTS

DAWN AND DARK

GOD with His million cares
    Went to the left or right,
Leaving our world; and the day
    Grew night.

Back from a sphere He came
    Over a starry lawn,
Looked at our world; and the dark
    Grew dawn.

A

A SHILLING EACH

How shall a man or woman pass unstirred?
A shilling these! One shilling, cage and bird!

I vow to birds my pennies! I will pinch,
Redeeming redstart, yellowhammer, finch.

Let them recover all their greens and blues!
Threadbare my coat shall be and old my shoes.

O sweet to fill my hand with living fluff,
And toss the loves to heaven—joy enough!

Give me to kiss each shining head; to feel
The wild-bird in the captive make appeal.

Suffer my cheek, O blackbird, on your breast,
Then slip to Laura's bosom for a nest;

Her lips must gently consecrate your flight—
Dear bird, she kisses you. Good-night, good-night!

Behold my darling's orchard for your bill !
Peck here in peace and take your fruity fill.

No kin of mine shall cheat you of the blue
And keep my love and Laura's ; nor shall you

Feel grip of Christmas hunger, for a tithe
Of all our bread shall help you that you thrive.

My heart has ached to see your duller eye
Watching the greedy city hurry by.

On Laura's breast at evening I have heard
A heart beat pity for the prisoned bird ;

And we have vowed to spend with care ; to pinch
For linnet, lark and starling, thrush and finch.

To throw these loves to heaven with a kiss,
Blue-ward and sun-ward—that shall be our bliss.

Faded is Laura's homespun, if you will—
The woodland knows a once familiar bill!

What need to care for shabbiness that shows?
A shilling redstart perches on her rose!

Children of men and brothers of my day,
How long shall feathered joy be thrust away

To find a foot of prison, smoky air
For that large liberty and country fare

Which tenderness celestial set apart
For woodlark wings and velvet whitethroat heart?

How shall a man or woman pass unstirred?
A shilling these!   One shilling, cage and bird!

A COTSWOLD VILLAGE

Roses !

Great wild roses,

Aisles of bud and whitethroat song

All along

The lower lanes

Where Peace,

That first inhabitant of earth,

Remains :

Folding her hands as day begins

And closes

She, tranquil, watches May

That melts to June in roses,

Great wild roses,

Roses !

These are so fair that they should rest

My rivals on the snowdrop breast

Where God, by some sweet circle of event,

Has lent me refuge when I turn

From street and stool

And work by rule,

Scarred by the plea of endless discontent,

The wine of morning sunshine stale or spent.

We neither spoke.

The leafy lyrics of the stripling oak

Sang us along.

Hamlet by hamlet passed,

And yellow sheep,

We came at last

Upon the hills that keep,

As mothers watch their babes asleep,

Long Compton guarded in the vale:
There as a dreaming child it lay
And took the evening light;
It was the vocal end of day
And larks in giddy flight
So out of view made music ring
That clouds, not birds,
Appeared to sing.

Go home, go home, ye doves, from out the field!
Fly to your forest cradles, fly!
In ambuscades of greenery concealed
Ponder the day gone by.
The shepherd is gone home,
The last rooks come,

Dear Jenny Wren shall whistle nothing more;

His team well-housed and fed

The ploughman thinks of bed,

And smiles upon his sweetheart at the door.

Down Gipsy Lane we roam,

Go home, ye doves, go home!

Little of sunlight now

This fruitful valley holds,

Deeper the greys invade,

Fainter become the golds;

The youngling's tap is on the pane,

And maids with sewing mothers sigh;

Go home, go home, ye doves, from out the field,

To forest cradles fly!

We walked toward the inn.

O host and hostess looking forth

To make the welcome warm,

What man may fare from south to north,

From palace or from farm,

Shall early learn your kindly hearts

And never come to harm!

O happy days!

O days of country beauty made more sweet

By steppings of dear feet

And voices captured from the city's stress

To add a charm to all the loveliness

Of leaf and land!

The lesser whitethroat in the orchard growth

Beneath an apple planned

A hive for nest,

And as we lay and watched

The while she matched

Each grassy joist and beam,

The fluffy architect, unstirred,

Rounded the entrance with her beak

Or smoothed the cup

Where she would dream

Upon her family of eggs,

And warm them into song

Where pears and pippins throng.

Early we rose and raced to catch

Initial glories of the morn;

The air itself was an embrace,

And Beauty, living in the place,

Seemed growing personal and kind,

Till in my heart,

Till on my face

I felt the thrill

That comes when lips I love consent,

Obedient to my will.

So hour by hour and day by day

Long Compton nursed our idleness,

Each meadow-path, each woodland way

Where campion calls and bluebells press

Conferred its bounty of delight ;

And when the fields of heaven were bright

With stars that have a native fire,

And those that do conspire

To rob a sun,

We knew a lane

Where in a briar's heart a bird

Released a strain

To cheer the mother musing on her eggs,

And promise her a son

Whose tender tale

Should shake the sleeping rosebud into dreams

And be the wonder of this Cotswold vale.

When time is weary of my company

Here let me rest.

If I should end within four walls

With bricks around,

Buy me no smoky patch of city ground,

But bring me to these acres of repose

Whose natural consecration is most sure,

That I may sleep beneath a country rose

·And where the dew is pure;

For in this valley God appeared to me,

And where my soul is let my body be.

What time the Father walked His earth

He trod, I know, these Cotswold slopes;

With silence and with sound

He clothed each mound;

The shadow of His robe goes over them,

The bounties of His wisdom cover them

And whoso cometh here

To tread this sod—

He sees the neighbour neighbourly,

And learning all Long Compton's loveliness

The better learns his God.

WAGES

My lass, when God
   To suffer sent me,
No gifts He gave,
   But only lent me
For gold, my breath,
   For silver, labour;
The sky as friend,
   The grass as neighbour.

The Vineyard called
   For workers many;
At eve I took
   God's punctual penny:
Because I bowed
   Content, I fancy
He gave me you
   For wages, Nancy!

PIGEONS AT CANNON STREET

O YE pigeons of the Station with your sorcery
Of hues,
Some in opal tints resplendent, some in filmy fluff of
Blues,
As ye circle dearly downward, peck the cabmen's
Alms, unshot,
I could think you living colours falling on this dull
Stone plot.

Here, the friends of men and horses, ye serenely find
Your food,
Ev'ry happy mother bringing sons and daughters from
Her brood;
Rough the act and strange the tumult that can stir you
From your rest,
Making all the yard a rainbow with the light of wing
And breast.

Ye are birds in Babylon whose sires were babies in
The tree;
Once the bright eyes of your nation saw beneath
Them romp in glee
Little roes that chased the fawns, and tusky boars that
Stabbed the dog
Where the lovely leagues of azure sparkled innocent
Of fog.

Tho' the wilderness of mortar, tho' the miles of brick
And slate
Dawn by dawn are seen for ever as the comrades of
Your fate,
In the fairy tales of pigeons, in the folk-songs, in
The lore
Are not green and grassy counties mingled sweetly as
Of yore?

Surely when the windy gods come roaring from the
Sea and wold

Creeping closely to some elder ye will ask him tales
Of old—

How the piping shepherd gathered all his lambs at
Death of light;

How the fields were fat with increase; how the
Were-wolf snarled at night.

London pigeons, many brothers, many sisters have
I seen

Flying woodward in the evening to their palaces
Of green;

Tho' I closelier scan your feathers more I love the
Wild surprise

Of your Warwickshire relations mounting sudden to
The skies.

O the peaty moorland odours and the sparkling sweep
Of lawn!
O the last thin shade of darkness melting on the lips
Of dawn!
These are gifts of God your kindred spy and ponder
From their trees
While the mower's scythe is making golden haloes
Round his knees!

'Twixt the rows of mangel-wurzels, strutting stately, I
Can see
Careful cousins pecking, wary, ready for the hill
Or tree;
Ye, methinks, have lost your birthright, lost your
Heritage of dew,
Lost the verdant county acres and the freedom of
The blue!

PARTING

Why, love, don't weep !
  Our joy was long,
Sweet twenty years
  Of smile and song.
I shall but wait
  Asleep, asleep,
For you to come—
  Why, love, don't weep !

Why, love, don't weep !
  The end is this ;
There comes a bound
  To speech and kiss :
For joy like ours
  The price is cheap—
Sweet twenty years !
  Why, love, don't weep !

A FAREWELL

GOOD-BYE, little maid,

You 're too old for my knee!

You are dressed in a frock 'tis a torture to see;

And the skirt has invaded

The hose which concealed

The limbs that went twinkling

From forest to field.

But a week, and I saw a sweet flash of your knee

As you jumped at the brook

In a moment of daring,

Not thinking of, caring

For sudden concealment

Of virgin revealment.

And now in a dress 'tis a torture to see

They will teach you to smirk

And to ogle, and be

But a bait for the wealthy,

The wolfish and stealthy

Who buy a young girl at a fabulous fee.

For the man who is poor—

For my heart—you will be

Unapproachable She!

In a year you will blush

If I speak of your rush

At the brook and the fence,

And with tutored pretence

Talk the tattle that grows at an afternoon tea!

Alas for the gossiping, tremulous tree

Which you mounted to loot;

Till, afar in the green,

Brightly golden, was seen

The head that I loved so, the fairest of fruit!

No more shall I follow, no more shall you flee,

For now, in a dress 'tis a torture to see,

You who were yesterday

Wild as a finch

They gird and be-pinch.

Farewell to the days when your tresses were free—

Good-bye, little maid,

You 're too old for my knee !

GOING SOUTH

IT is ever so far away
  For the swallow to fly;
And she peeped from an English thatch
  At a round of sky!

But the elders have told her tales
  Of the sister blues;
And she starts at the wink of dawn
  On her windy cruise.

She can tell her path in the void,
  Though her native sod
Was here in a Warwickshire lane;
  For her pilot's God.

AN ORCHARD DANCE

ALL work is over at the farm

And men and maids are ripe for glee;

Love slips among them sly and warm

Or calls them to the chestnut-tree.

As Colin looks askance at Jane

He draws his hand across his mouth;

She understands the rustic pain,

And something of the tender south

About her milkmaid beauty flits.

Her dress of lilac print for guide

Draws shepherd Colin where she sits,

Who, faring to her lovely side

To snatch his evening pension tries,

But skimming like a bird from clutch

The maid escapes his Cupid touch,

And speeding down a passage flies

Not fast enough to cheat his eyes.
Ah, sweet-lip ways and sweet-lip days,
And sweetheart captures of the waist,
How swiftly still the virgin runs
She 's sure at last to be embraced !
Now Colin fires at kiss delayed,
And faster flits the red stone floor
Till Fortune yields the tricky maid
A captive at the pantry door !

The farmer with his fifty years
Is not too old to join the fun ;
He pulls the milkmaids' pinky ears
And bids a likely stripling run
To find the fiddlers for a dance :
And in the cherry orchard there

A tune shall mingle with romance,
And love be brave in open air.

The village wakens to the bliss,
The crones and gaffers crawl to see
The country game of step and kiss
Beneath the laden cherry-tree.
The chairs and benches now are set,
Old John is wheedled from his pet,
The cider cup with beady eyes
Responds to winkings of the skies.
The farmer, burly in his chair,
Now claps for ev'ry fond and fair
To foot it on the grassy patch
While rustic violinists snatch
From out those varnished birds of wood

27

A tune to jink it in the blood.

Now Jane and Colin in a trice

Float sweetly round not less than thrice

Before their motion draws a pair

To revel with the dancing air.

The thrush, that on his velvet wipes

His juicy bill, protesting pipes,

And; somewhat as a piccolo,

Doth race the concord of the bow.

A virgin yonder by the tree

Rejects a mate who saucily

Would press, if she might only start,

Her modest homespun to his heart.

Ah, sweet-lip ways and sweet-lip days,

And sweetheart captures of the waist,

Though like a finch the maiden flies

She's sure at last to be embraced.

The orchard now is in full bloom
With rosy cheek and snowdrop throat;
The stars invade the growing gloom,
And rarelier sounds the blackbird's note.
But in this dewy little park
Love burns the brighter for the dark,
And till he use a stricter rule
Dear Cicely's cheek shall never cool!
The fiddlers storm a tomboy tune,
The shepherds closer clasp the girls
While skirts the more desert the shoon,
And rebel leap the lovely curls.
The farmer glows within his chair
And muses on the dancing time

When he and She—a matchless pair—
Were warm and nimble in their prime.
God bless the man who, duller grown,
Can feel the younger heaven anew
By granting to his maids and men
A romp by starlight in the dew !
Ah, greenwood ways and greenwood days,
And soft pursuings of the waist,
The cheek must yellow out of praise,
And bent be those who once embraced !

And now they pant against the trees,
And, using darkness for their plan,
Girls loose the garters at their knees
And mend the clumsiness of man.
One virgin, thankful for the dance,

About the music shyly trips—

Her Love 's a fiddler, and her love

Pops fruit in Paganini's lips;

Or finding on the starlit tree

The wife and husband cherry there,

She hangs the couple at his cheek

And hides the stalk with tufts of hair.

The girls are at the cider-cup,

And shepherds tilt the yellow base

Until a giddy amber flood

Runs, kissing, over Cicely's face,

And Dora's upper lip doth shine

With winking beads of apple-wine.

The fiddlers scrape a farewell tune,

The dancers dwindle in the dusk

While summer puffs of easy wind

Bring hints of cottage garden musk.

And thus the revel dearly ends
With milkmaid's palm in shepherd's hand,
And lovers grow from only friends
Where plum and pear and apple stand.
Ah, sweet-lip ways and sweet-lip days,
And sweetheart captures of the waist,
How fast so-e'er the virgin flies
She's sure at last to be embraced!

DELIA

Delia, that will not kiss,
    Is hardly ripe
To glow again at airs
    Of shepherd-pipe.
Sing of the flock to-day,
    And wait for Love
To storm the simple breast,
    And stir the dove.

Touch but her tender waist
    And she shall cry!
But Love may come before
    Her tears are dry.
Then, shepherd, tune to trees
    Your wanton pipe;
Delia, that will not kiss,
    Is hardly ripe.

C

IN PAIN

PAIN is the language of decay,
The tongue of human impotence;
It waits upon our coming here,
Our going hence,
Implacably austere:
And from our earliest breath,
Which is the birth of death,
A soft-foot mute
It seems to prophesy a coming sleep,
Another sphere.

Long have I journeyed thro' the Great Fatigue
Of life.
Lo, I have had my share of grass and birds—
And strife.
For me has Pain, the sentinel,
Been vigilant

To pace my plot and dwell

Within my tent;

Oft in the night with small alarms

Has stirred me out of rest,

Alert, oppressed,

Till shepherded within thine arms

And on thy breast,

O loving Lady, in the curse of Pain

I have been blest—

Have felt soft hands rebuke the agony

And stroke my face

With fingers that are ministers of love,

Ambassadors of peace

To bring release

For that sharp prisoned pain along my brow

As, would to God, they brought it, Lady, now!

BABY

Come, Mother, bring the baby out,
    And let her roll—the grass is dry !
Take off her shoes, and she shall kick
    Those pinky toes toward the sky.

The firmament forgive her crime !
    And as a sign of love and grace
May God, who holds it, send my child
    Her mother's hair, her mother's face !

See, Mary, here's a cherry-tree
    To make her eyes grow round and bright ;
Oh, how she chatters to the fruit—
    The dimpled bundle of delight !

There, sweetheart ! See the gaudy cheek,
    And see the naughty lurking stone ;
And now each juicy half (my word !)
    Is Baby Rosebud's very own !

Dear Mother, as I watch this child
  Stare upward to the depthless blue,
My spirit, fleeter than the gaze,
  Goes up with thanks for her and you.

God, blight my orchard, scourge my friend,
  And drive my blackbird from his tree,
But leave this babe for Mary's breast,
  And let me tend them both for Thee!

FATHER THRUSH

THE thrush was a bachelor early in March,
And now there's a wife with a velvety heart;
    There's a house in the quick
    Never builded of brick
And a capital egg for a start.

The thrush was a bachelor early in March,
And now there's a medley of bosom and bill!
    There are Susan and Dick
    In the daggers of quick,
And a couple of golden-throats still!

A WALK

Cow-Honeybourne, that dost survey
The profile of that great green range
So seeming near, so far away,
It was from out thy sleepy heart
My friend and I did start
To tramp toward the temple of the hills,
Past poising hawks, past little gossip rills,
To storm the Cotswolds, and enjoy thereon
The fine frugality of winter sun.

The great tit in the apple-tree
Delayed us long ;
The shrill staccato song
The creeper chirped amid his industry
Drew us from pollard unto pollard, till

We drank our fill

Of that white-feathered patch, his breast,

His busy bill

That with detective skill

Stabbed at each crevice in the wood

In search of food.

'Twas through an orchard valley that we passed,

And all the pear-tree boles were painted white;

Small wonder if the pinky maid,

A kiss half-melted on her lips,

Should shrink at night

When not embraced

About her waist

By Dick the ploughman's arm,

For very ghostly in the gloom

These whitened files of pear-trees loom

Beside the farm.

We marched toward the succour of the hills,

And came to Weston at the middle day.

We hymned the rural loveliness

With glowing words,

And made response with clumsy human lips

To all the easy chattering of the birds.

The hedge's darkly purple top

We praised;

The verdure of the coming crop;

The glazed

And glorious bulwark of the beach;

The wind that with clear Cotswold speech

Addressed the poplar gustily—

The poplar that would rather be

A spire to pierce the blue

Than lend its secret energy

To grow

In liberal breadth below.

The lane that led us upward now was steep,

And slowlier we stept.

Oh, how the peace of God was there,

And how the country slept!

Ten leagues away the city's filth

That gnaws our faculties by stealth,

And we were free!

Men flying from our slavery!

Nothing between our lowliness

And God on high !

Here in this pure encampment of repose

The grass can see the sky,

And all the acres of exceeding blue

Look down upon the dew ;

No hell of uncongenial fog

Can come betwixt these two.

We stood upon the forehead of the hills,

And lifted up our hearts in prayer ;

And as we halted, reverent,

Meseemed that Nature o'er us bent,

That she did bid us sup

From bread she gave and from her cup.

There at her large communion did we feast,

Herself the Substance and herself the Priest.

The immaterial wine she poured,

And standing on the Cotswold sward

Administered to us

Beneath the unsupported sky

Her sacrament of scenery.

Thus made her child, I inly felt

Her gradual unction me possess;

Accumulated baseness melt,

And such behaviour press

Into my life as shall invoke

The rainbow to the street,

Green grasses for my feet

Unseen by blinder folk;

And leave me heir to some supreme content

Until, O Friend, with you

I drink anew

On Cotswold hills of Nature's sacrament.

CONVALESCENCE

THREE weeks her face was snowy white
  From memory of her pain,
But then, with dear, recapturing light
  A gradual glow again

Taught almost tintless buds to show
  Their mimicry of pink;
They were but ghosts of former glow,
  But yet a lovely link

Between the opulence of health,
  The poverty of care,
When she but grew my greater wealth,
  And fathomlessly fair.

At last the happy edict gave
  A boundary to alarms,
And lifting her, myself the slave,
  Heaven trembled in my arms!

Now wife and babe before my fire

In speechless converse rest;

The milky comfort, his desire,

And hers, the bounteous breast.

One arm is free, and strong with joy

Around me warmly slips

When that I stoop to bless the boy,

And touch him with my lips.

TO ORANGES

Ye thousand yellow worlds from Spain

Upon a barrow piled,

And bartered for the timid pence

Of some desirous child,

How do your smooth and shining spheres

Recall the years

When by that sunny inland sea

I dreamed great dreams that may not be

Translated to reality !

Throughout the gradual day

Ye fade away

As dreams.

Hoarsely the invitation of your master goes

Adown the street ;

With careless, cunning hand he throws

To children's innocence
Some value for their pence ;
And his proud pyramid of fruit
From apex unto base descends ;
Each golden atom blends
With all the large and general life
That throbs through London strife.

Ye ride to far suburban homes
In Juliet's very cosy muff—
The one that cousin Herbert gave,
All wonder, warmth, and fluff !
The haggard merchant rushing by
Thinks sweetly of his nursery
Where Ralph and Jenny watch the rain
Becloud the pane.

If he should miss the train !

The Coster, cordial, winks ;

God bless the babes, the merchant thinks,

If I should lose the six

There 's one at seven,

And these will make a little heaven

For those two angels whom I love !

Off goes his glove !

Out comes a threepenny bit !

And the abysses of the bag are lit

By leaping rounds of yellow rain—

Soft tumbling circles fresh from Spain !

O Spanish captives in the Strand

That pour the south along the street,

A man in pleasantness may stand
And read your history awhile ;
Thus ye have made me smile,
And made me sigh,
For as ye go, go I.
My pyramid of hours grows less,
Fewer the lips that laugh,
The hands that bless,
And rarely comes the greeting kind
To make my heart the quicklier beat.
I am not fruit, but rind,
O sweet barbarians of the street,
That, severed from your native land,
Do pour the south
Along the Babel length of Strand !

A PASTORAL

Come you, Mary, there 's a dear!

  Mind no more the plaguy dairy!

Milk can never match your white—

    Come you, Mary!

All the music of my scythe

  Sang you in the heated meadow;

And I thought your shape behind

    Ev'ry shadow!

Down with sleeves, and bring those lips

  (Roseleaves in the happy dairy)

To the chestnut where we kiss—

    Come you, Mary!

THE NIGHTINGALE

WHEREAS the blackbird and the thrush
    Are fondly English in their song,
And finely pipe great island airs
    Where bloomy orchards throng,

The nightingale has all the East
    Within his dear tumultuous breast;
World-passions and the strong refrains
    That ring in wild unrest.

Circassian music he can sing,
    Rough mountain loves, and stories meek
That in the vineyard valley run
    From traitor cheek to cheek.

And all the secrets of desire,
    By right of lyric ancestry,
From out a midnight hawthorn bush
    He now reveals to me.

AT BRANDON

On the ivied house the starling
  Clapped his beak as we went by,
And the dipping chaffinch flying
  Slipped in loops across the sky.
Here and there a hermit poplar
  Musing on his stature stood,
And we heard, advancing farther,
  Unseen wings within the wood.
What a lesson is the forest
  For a brotherhood of life !
What a green rebuke for nations
  Ever ready for the strife !
Here within a space no longer
  Than a blackbird floats unfanned,
Oak and elm and beech, the chieftains,
  Spire in peace above the land.

Here we heard the windy shepherd

   Making cloudy lambkins pass

Over Nature's pupils dreaming

   With their mistress in the grass.

As we lay a stockdove fluttered,

   Settled on a branch in view,

And we saw her comely plumpness

   Lined against the evening blue,

Till she spied beneath her pouting

   Shapes that are the pulse of flight—

Thought us enemies, and melted

   Very softly out of sight

Westward, where a wall of blackness

   Stood before a yellow lake,

While along the inky summit

   Crawled a great and golden snake!

Here we heard the whitethroats homing
From the raiding of the day;
Heard the prophet thrush proclaiming
Divination from his spray.

Bringing back his song from spaces
Where the world is faintly seen
To his field the lark descended,
Seeking slumber in the green.

Multitudes of gossip creatures
Darkness gathered to repose;
But we drank of Nature's silence
Till the huntress moon arose—

Till Diana, lap and bosom
Finely full of stolen light,
By her beautiful unbending
Made a lover of the night.

A PRAYER

TEND me my birds, and bring again
   The brotherhood of woodland life,
So shall I wear the seasons round,
   A friend to need, a foe to strife.

Keep me my heritage of lawn,
   And grant me, Father, till I die
The fine sincerity of light
   And luxury of open sky.

So, learning always, may I find
   My heaven around me everywhere,
And go in hope from this to Thee,
   The pupil of Thy country air.

AT MIDNIGHT

Now that the living sleep
   And the dead awake,
Joy shall return to me
   And my cold hands take.

Here at the midnight hour
   I shall feel again
Love in a kiss, and then
   The resulting pain.

But when the dawn shall speed
   With its stealth and flash,
Deep in my heart the fire
   Shall again be ash.

A PASTORAL

WHO would shepherd pipes forsake
    If there greet him dearly
Cupid in the knee-deep brake
    Singing sweet and clearly?
Who to London deserts go,
    Scanning friendless faces,
If there beat a heart for him
    Under Laura's laces?

As I near the leafy oak,
    Laura, swift as starling,
Brings her cheek for me to stroke—
    Little fragrant darling!
Take your air in Rotten Row,
    Gentlemen of leisure,
Milkmaid kiss and velvet sloe
    Fashion me my pleasure!

While we sit the stilly skies
  Change from blue to purple,
And my arm in daring lies
  Round a homespun circle!
Thus doth pastoral delight
  Follow shepherd-duty,
Speeding to my heart at night
  Laura's love and beauty!

Good it is when Northern winds come blowing from
    the ice and bear,
Shouting round the shaking steeple till the opal stars
    can hear ;
Good it is in shifting dusks to feel the polar thunder-
    flail
Lashing at the weary forehead with its knots of biting
    hail !

Hurricanes that blow the foxes over leagues towards
    their prey,
Roaring sagas of the icebergs, songs of baby seals at
    play !
Hurricanes with ghostly chorus of the Norsemen grim
    and stark
Hurling oaths at giant foemen hacking furious in the
    dark !

In the lulls between the wrangle of the tempest and
the floe

Sweet it is to fancy love-songs of the patient Es-
quimaux ;

Speeding, warm at heart, across the level purity of
plain,

Love beneath his furs as constant as beneath the ice
the main !

Oh, I joy to hear the sinews of the god of Northern
blast

Crackle as his fingers fasten on the icy hilt and vast !

Rushing over wold and valley, dusky dells and uplands
bleak,

How he flings his frozen gauntlet at the challenge of
my cheek !

Tho' he dash the dew about me from the blooms of
other stars,

Pansies from the lap of Venus, speary rushes down
from Mars,

More I love his gusty onset than the woman-breeze
· that brings

Scent of harems and the radiant Persian roses on his
wings !

Northland god, your tears of fury drive upon my
freshened cheeks,

While the roadside branch above me writhes in agony
and creaks !

As we wrestle at the midnight, breast to breast and
hand to hand,

Care and pain depart like swallows lifting to a friendly
land !

THE FIRST KISS

On Helen's heart the day were night!
　　But I may not adventure there:
Her breast is guarded by a right,
　　And she is true as fair.

And though in happy days her eyes
　　The glow within mine own could please,
She's purer than the babe who cries
　　For empire on her knees.

Her love is for her lord and child,
　　And unto them belongs her snow;
But none can rob me of her wild
　　Young kiss of long ago!

A WISH

When I am done with pen and ink,
   And only sleep in careless hope,
Oh, bear me to the Cotswold hills
   And leave me on the southern slope!

The modesty of Nature glows
   And mingles with the country air;
The peace of God is on the land,
   And passeth understanding there.

Come, sweet and dearest, nor deny
   The tribute of one gentle pain;
Refresh my primrose with a tear;
   But never wish me home again.

TO MY BROTHERS

O BROTHERS, who must ache and stoop
   O'er wordy tasks in London town,
How scantly Laura trips for you—
   A poem in a gown!
How rare if Grub-street grew a lawn!
   How sweet if Nature's lap could spare
A dandelion for the Strand,
   A cowslip for Mayfair!

But here, from immaterial lyres,
   There rings in easy confidence
The blackbirds' bright philosophy
   On apple-spray or fence:
For ploughmen wending home from toil
   Some patriot thrush outpours his lay,
And voices, wildly eloquent,
   The diary of his day.

E

These living lyrics you may hear

 Remembering the lane's romance,

All hung in wicker hells to chirp

 Thin ghosts of utterance :

But where the gusts of liberty

 Make Ragged Robin wisely bend

They quicken hedgerows with their song,

 Melodiously unpenned.

If souls of mighty singers leave

 The vacant body to its hush,

Does Shelley linger in the lark,

 Or Keats possess the thrush?

The end is undecaying doubt,

 And in some blackbird's bosom still

Great Tennyson may sweeten eve

 And whistle on the hill.

Come, brothers, to this clean delight,
   And watch the velvet-headed tit.
Here's honest sorrel in the grass
   And sturdy cuckoo-spit :
What shepherds hear you shall not miss,
   And at deliverance of dawn
Shall see a miracle of bloom
   Across the sparkling lawn.

The forest musically begs
   To fan you with its leafy love ;
Oh, fall asleep upon this moss
   Entreated by the dove !
Here shall that sweet Conservative,
   Dear Mother Nature, lend to you
Her lovely rural elements
   Beneath the primal blue.

O brothers, who must ache and stoop
  O'er wordy tasks in London town,
How scantly Laura trips for you—
  A poem in a gown !
How good if Fleet-street grew a lawn !
  How sweet if garden-plots could spare
A bed of cloves to scent the Strand,
  A pansy for Mayfair !

THE BUDDING OF THE ORCHARD

Oh! the budding of the orchard
    Is a heralding of June;
Of the woodlark's brighter bosom,
    And the freedom of her tune.
In the hedge's heart the sparrow
    Tends her sapphire eggs in love
Till the song that's in the oval
    Makes a music for the grove.
And the grass beside the river
    Grows the long cool green of joy
For the creature in its comfort,
    And the maiden and the boy.

Oh! the budding of the orchard
    Is a promise to my hope

Of the grey and opal evening
  Over lambs upon the slope.
I shall see the stock and pansy
  And the brown of Cicely's arm ;
I shall hear the harness tinkle,
  And the cattle at the farm :
And the God above my forehead
  In his camp of beam and blue
For the colony of rosebuds
  Shall remember drops of dew.

HAPPY LIFE

Baby beauty on my knee,
    Baby's mother near me;
Master Bullfinch grown so tame
    That he cannot fear me;
Brooks to tell of dipping maids,
    Ruby cloves to scent me—
What a happy, happy life
    God in trust has lent me!

Baby tumbles on our bed,
    Either cheek a cherry,
Raiding Laura's lovely heart,
    Mischievous and merry!
Infant swallows at my eaves
    Twitter, and content me—
What a happy, happy life
    God in trust has lent me!

INSPIRATION

I LAY my head on the foolscap page,
  Bidden to sing, and being mute;
No help there came with the lovely air
  Of the blackbird's magic flute.

My Love ran in, and she kissed my cheek.
  Lyrics woke in my blood and rang;
Her hair glowed gold by the foolscap page,
  And the barren singer sang.

TO DORA

God's mercy, Dora, what's a kiss

   That you should whimper like a child?

A maid was ne'er as coy as this,

   A woodlark never was so wild.

There went, i' faith, no niggard pinch

You little pecking sweetbill finch!

Come, loveliness, 'tis but the task

   Of mating Cupid's red to red;

A rosebud touch is all I ask,

   Lift up, dear nun, this shining head!

There I see how good a thing it is—

God's mercy, Dora, what's a kiss?

CLARINDA'S BEAUTY

THE tree may win the stripling
  With its clusters round and red,
And a shepherdess may languish
  Till his silly mouth is fed;
But Clarinda has an orchard
  Where sweet circles grow for me,
And no shepherd, though he covet,
  Dares approach my cherry-tree!

The mistress airs her velvet
  Ev'ry Sunday down the aisle
As the sunburnt farmers titter,
  And the saucy milkmaids smile;
Though it cost a mort of money
  And can make the children stare,
'Tis a thistle to the softness
  That Clarinda's cheek doth wear.

But when my sweetheart dangles

    In the Avon as it goes

Her feet, and cattle ponder

    On the marvel of her hose,

Not a virgin ever trusted

    Such a comely white as this

To the chilly river fingers,

    And for water-lips to kiss!

REGRET

O HUMAN bird, whose nest has been

Within my heart a thousand days,

To fly away so suddenly

When April glittered in her green,

And woodland aisles

For leafy miles

In fifty fine harmonious ways

Were musical with flying praise,

Was a strange winging from my life,

O false and fair—

Was a departure that the sense

Could nowhere gather strength to bear!

Day comes.

The Artist of the dawn

Makes all the sky a masterpiece;

The dewdrops vanish from the lawn

And from the shepherd's sheep.

Each day 's a miracle to cheat the mind,

Night brings the wonder, sleep ;

But all along the lane there flies

My loss of her whose helping eyes

Made olden moments kind ;

And in the pulsing heart of night,

When darkness seems to throb to light,

Remembrance of my whitethroat yet

Comes with a great regret.

No blackbird's magic in the bush,

Succeeded by the aching hush,

Can win me from my thought of her ;

And all that Father Avon says

To leagues of blue forget-me-nots

Cannot cast out

My dream of Jenny's girlish ways,

Her lovely pout;

And all those perished days

When on my knees

She sat contented till the sun was set—

God has not fashioned me to think them nought,

Or taught me to forget!

HANNIBAL, SAGUNTO CAPTO, LOQUITUR.

THANKS to your pith Saguntum is destroyed!

'Tis time to pipe the songs of Carthage now;

To muse upon the world within its streets,

The tinkling in some soft and sandy place

Of camel cavalcades whose spicy loads

Make fragrant leagues for those who march behind.

The Gods are gracious.   I enrich you all

With pastoral dawns and twilights of repose.

Go, make the girdled hearts revolt with joy,

And feel around your necks the arms of peace;

Hide in the sheath that gapped and greedy blade

That drank the plenty of Saguntum veins!

What of the siege, my heroes?   Was it long?

What of the sack, my heroes?   Was it good?

Each sword has won a virgin; ev'ry man

White witching arms to tie him round with love.

Has not the wine run freely in the camp,

Or have I niggardly denied the can

Its island-cluster of canary beads

That hissed and bridled, sparkling as you roared

Great soldier-songs that rumbled in the hills?

Your beards are hung with purple dewdrops yet,

Drops of the wine that splashed the naked knees

Of girls who speed it round your garrulous fires.

Take back this history of roaring fight,

Take home your scars to Carthage; show the trench

Saguntum bullies carved upon your cheeks,

Till youths, midway between the boy and man,

Shall itch to glut beside their country's sons

A thirsty blade throughout our next campaign,

And maidens sing you in their fountain-songs.

Oh, how the dame's recovered cheek will flush

At news of hostile handiwork; to learn

Her husband's mightier arm confused the foe!

Your sons will reap incentives, and each wound

Will be a star to guide the coming brood

To follow glory upward to a scar.

The striplings of the land will charge at play

With girlish swords and baby javelins;

Their harmless bows will speed as harmless shafts.

'Tis thus the glamour grows; for stirring tales

Of onset, and the death-grip day by day,

Of peril, rescue, booty and applause

Are trumpets to the blood and signals fine

To urge the sprouting heroes of our kin.

I am a man of battle, and I yearn

To see young tigers lap their early blood,

So here I make a harvest of my plans

And loot the hours of possible design.

Gods, if the soul of Carthage should not feel

That glory waiting past the Pyrenees—

Should dwindle to a passive, womanish thing,

And, barren, shirk the dominating task!

But when your stiffened fingers scarce stretch out

For gripping iron handles, it is ill

To let the shadow of another war

Fall thus athwart your pleasure. Let me hope.

Home to the mellow homeland songs and dance,

For standards, scars upon your daring cheeks!

O for a sight of Carthage ! Homing braves,

I charge you bear me when the Spring's at bud

Sweet gossip of my mistress and my wife!

She sits eternal by the lusting sea

And stares upon the wilderness of blue,

Kept by the beating of a million hearts!

Within her gates unrivalled maidens blush

Whose necks are clasped by chiming ornaments;

They look to Spain, and supplicate the Gods

To bring you home to kisses from the war.

Go, dream beside their beauty!   Go, and take

The throbbing sweethearts in your potent arms—

Arms that can help an empire to be set,

Babe of an empire, in this Spanish West.

Each with his lips against some sleeping cheek

Forget the clank of armour and the shrill

Quick scream of arrows, and the wind

The stone makes coming from the monstrous sling;

But when the branch begins to feel the leaf

At push and pout in her, forsake those lips

Are rivals of your greatness, and arise!

Your road is Spain-wards! Once again
Intrust you to the mouthings of the deep,
Placating first, by prayers and gifts of worth,
The sea-god looking through his opal roof.
Come back to me with even sharper swords,
And not one pinch of all the excellence
You showed of old lost in the realm of ease,
Forgetting not the soul of all my need
Sweet gossip of my mistress and my wife—
Carthage I took in trust from Hasdrubal,
Carthage I widen, love, and glorify.
So, with good news of her, and you in trim
To swing her steel as strongly as of old,
I doubt not we shall fright the Eagle yet,
And pour our language through the streets of Rome!

A CONTRAST

THE apple in my garden
 Is a round of bloom and scent,
With the grass beneath it pointing
 To the blue above it bent :
Here's dew of dawn, and music
 That can shame a city's rush ;
For Town the hurdy-gurdy,
 But for Warwickshire the thrush !

At middle day the blossom
 Takes the utmost of the sun ;
The tits as sweet explorers
 All along the branches run :
'Tis wild-birds' country piping
 That can make the forehead flush ;
For Town the hurdy-gurdy,
 But for Warwickshire the thrush !

As Mary milks the cattle,
  And I stoop to kiss her cheek,
The lilac shakes with lyrics
  From the song-bird's easy beak :
'Twas God who made him poet—
  How his masterpieces gush !
For Town the hurdy-gurdy,
  But for Warwickshire the thrush !

A SONG

ALL night I have lain in the Gipsies' camp,
    Heel to heel with a gipsy lass,
With a planet hung in the sky for lamp,
    And for bed the honest grass :
At morn I have wended upon my way,
    Taking only as baggage this—
The love that lies in a gipsy's eyes
    And a gipsy maiden's kiss.

All day I have pined for the greensward girl,
    Brown and sweet in the forest hush,
Where a man may play with a southland curl,
    And a southland virgin's blush :
I'd give my wealth if there warmed me again,
    Filling eve with a daring bliss,
The heart that pressed at a gipsy's vest,
    And a wildwood gipsy's kiss.

CICELY BATHING

THE brook told the dove
    And the dove told me
That Cicely's bathing at the pool
    With other virgins three.

The brook told the dove
    And the dove told me
That Cicely floating on the wave
    Woke music in the tree.

The brook told the dove
    And the dove told me
That Cicely's drying in the sun,
    A snowy sight to see.

HESTER SINCLAIR

HESTER SINCLAIR passed me by,
    Busy at her glove—
Hester Sinclair whom I call
    Lavender and love !

Little waves of muslin film
    Lapping at her feet,
Hester trips, all snow in snow,
    Country fair and sweet.

Hester Sinclair homes to me—
    Mine this woodland dove !
Hester trembles in my arms
    Lavender and love !

BETTER SO

FRIEND, you did well to die!

How agonising was that hour
When the last inch of candle grew
A heated pool; when at the pane
The morning wind, a bully, blew,
While you, no whit discomfited
By all these great Spring gusts at play,
In all the sorcery of senselessness
Did hardly stay
To breathe away
The fragments of your span,
Last lingerings of the man

So soon to fashion us supreme distress.

In the acacia on the lawn

The storm-cock whistled vengeance and disdain ;

The milder thrush, in harmony with fate,

Piped cheerly through the active flight of rain

Ineffably sedate.

Below him in the lilac-tree

The blackbird in his cottage green

Did sing between

The plainings and content.

O God, I thought, bring back again

His pleasure in the firmament ;

Instruct his ears to catch

Some redstart's whisper, some reviving snatch

Of chaffinch music, ere, the morning spent,

These servants of the dawn,

These breathing songs,

Desert the lawn!

His ears, O Lord, were reverent,

And Thou dost know

He loved Thy miracles

With all his force,

Praising Thee daily more because Thy love

Mellowed the woodland with the soothing dove,

Set linnets in the gorse,

Made sweet the darkness with the nightingale

That we might find his comfort in the vale

Though seeing not its source.

Give him to hear again our words,

To hear the birds;

To drink the landscape's distances

With those deep eyes

In ecstasies

At finding spread around him everywhere

The everlasting sameness and surprise.

Friend, you did well to die!

The incarnation of ideals

Is slow;

The health of nations mendeth not;

They go

From base to base

Immeasurably fraudulent

In gross and cunning government.

But you did burn to see

A Brotherhood arise

That in nobility should not misfit

.

The Maker of our skies;

But day by day more separate we stand,

Pursuing pelf,

Adoring self,

One blood, one fate, but not one Band.

Due to the spade and promised to the earth

We buy our guinea's worth of evening mirth,

Go home and ponder how the money spent

Shall be extorted from the negligent,

Improvident

Poor brother, who, with equal worth,

By all the devilry of biting need

Comes as a test of our prevailing creed

To beg, for Christ's sake, aid!

We, dressing for the tomb and promised to the

spade,

Make profit of his hurt

In golden dirt!

How this would wrench your heart if you were

    nigh,

You who with me

Could bear to see

Espousals of the brick and of the glade—

The serpent street crawl greedy to the wood,

The mason drive the pigeon from her bough,

The hind, dismayed,

From following his plough,

If all this robbery from Nature meant

A crop of fresh content;

If all these rendings of her verdant robe,

Invasions of her temples gave

Serener glory to the globe,

A thrilling to the slave!

Brother, they drive the field-mouse hence,

They steal the finches' home;

From mead to mead, from fence to fence,

With all the power of impotence

The merchant-princes come,

Sending the workmen first to clear the way,

To build and slay.

In half a hundred dingles where of yore

We lay on moss, and spake of Evermore

While blackbirds shrilled the present in our ears,

Are cots and babes and tears!

With moss and melody and woodlands dense

Fled Innocence,

As She will fly from centres of repose,

Northward and southward, east and west,

Within her bosom thrusting as She goes

Her honeysuckle and her pink wild-rose.

How this would wrench your heart if you were nigh!

Friend, it was well—that bitter vanishing—

Friend, you did well to die!

DORA'S RIBBON

PLAGUE upon the ribbon
   And the bow beneath my chin !
Bells no longer call me,
   And the service should begin.
Kate will walk with Colin,
   Mary go with John—
Drat the band of cherry silk
   That won't go on !

Plague upon the ribbon !
   I must fix it with a pin !
Yet the bow looks pretty
   As it cuddles at my chin !
Richard's in the garden
   Looking at my pane—
Sunday next the cherry band
   May sulk again !

COMFORT

How poorly reaches to my heart,
When all my joy is in eclipse,
The stilted comfort and the noise
Of kind, but useless, lips.

But down the road an arrow's flight
Where evening brings the sleepy birds,
The thinnest twitter in the green
Is more than clumsy words.

And in that forest synagogue,
Whose aisles are paved with bloom and sod,
A broken heart may haply find
The tenderness of God.

TO A GLOW-WORM

In thee there lives the energy
    Can make the turf a heaven,
May birds that peck thy candle die
    By Parson Rook unshriven!

Thou art a child the Father's hand
    Within this fruity acre
Dropt in the grass, as shy and still
    As any virgin Quaker!

Thou tiny, unofficial lamp
    Within my orchard burning,
Dost signal by this living star
    Thy husband home returning?

Here at this cherry's grassy base
    Thou'rt sure of no upbraiding;
Too small thy lantern to arouse
    The thrush for midnight raiding.

As tender girls at water-play

    Grow blanched when shepherds whistle,

So fades thy spark if carelessly

    I brush this neighbour thistle.

Ah, how my freckled lads would run,

    A knee apiece would capture,

And prattle questions if they watched

    Thy lovely light in rapture!

A SONG

It was the time when heaven comes down
And paves the wood with blue;
A firmament of hyacinths
Drank deep of forest dew:
The cooing of a lonely dove
Went mourning on the breeze,
And over all there swayed the songs
And sighings of the breeze.

The velvet palms of moss caressed
And comforted my face;
An angel joy from Paradise
Seemed truant in the place:
The forest was a voice, and sang,
O Love long dead, of you
What time the gracious heaven came down
And paved the wood with blue.

AT EVENING

BELOW her in the valley farm
   She heard the rustic mirth;
The pastures lessened to a line
   Was heaven as much as earth.

The fiddle poured a dancing tune,
   That called her feet.   And oh!
Her heart was hungry for the lad
   She danced with long ago!

OLD LETTERS

LAST night some yellow letters fell
  From out a scrip I found by chance;
Among them was the silent ghost,
  The spirit of my first romance:
And in a faint blue envelope
  A withered rose long lost to dew
Bore witness to the dashing days
  When love was large and wits were few.

Yet standing there all worn and grey
  The teardrops quivered in my eyes
To think of Youth's unshaken front,
  The forehead lifted to the skies;
How rough a hill my eager feet
  Flung backward when upon its crest
I saw the flutter of the lace
  The wind awoke on Helen's breast!

How thornless were the roses then

　　When fresh young eyes and lips were kind

When Cupid in our porches proved

　　How true the tale that Love is blind !

But Red-and-White and Poverty

　　Would only mate while shone the May ;

Then came a Bag of Golden Crowns

　　And jingled Red-and-White away. *

Grown old and niggard of romance

　　I wince not much at aught askew,

And often ask my favourite cat

　　What else had Red-and-White to do ?

And here's the bud that rose and sank,

　　A crimson island on her breast—

Why should I burn it ?　Once again

　　Hide, rose, and dream.　God send me rest.

MORNING

THE throstle and the dawn
Together come
That light and music may
Invade my home;

And wakefulness begins
In Laura's hands;
Upon her pillow stir
Those glowing strands

That lure me till I kiss
Her dreamy eyes
To win her back from sleep
To Paradise.

A LULLABY

SLEEP, dearest, sleep.

The birds are still,

The trees are hushed

Upon the hill.

Oh, in green dreamland valleys deep

Rest, dearest, rest—sleep, dearest, sleep.

Rest, Alice, rest,

And wait for me.

If Gods be kind

I come to thee!

Oh, in thine eyes the dawn is deep,

Rest, Alice, rest—sleep, Alice, sleep.

TO MY LOVE

(With a rose)

THAT freedom thou dost now control
   Once basely commerced with my soul;
All inward enterprise, unchid,
   In fancy grew as Fancy bid;
But now, possessed by thee, it grows
So clean a captive as this rose.

A DEFENCE

(Written on being charged with undue frankness)

DEAR country Muse, my heart's delight,
    Whose purity displays
The rounded nude of loveliness
    For shepherd-pipes to praise—

Dear Muse, that dancing on the green
    Inspired my country tone,
Have I who saw your chastity
    In seeing lost my own?

Have I, for all your liberal love
    And wildflower music, taught
A multitude your bosom's white
    Uncovered, but unsought—

And not this lesson from your snow,
    This knowledge from your knee—
That more of virtue, less of robe,
    Belongs to purity?

With glimpses of a sunny neck,
   And ripe untrespassed lips
That boasted even brighter red
   Than any autumn hips,

Barefooted, in a rebel robe
   That kissed your careless knee
And showed the splendour of your shape
   With woodland modesty,

You danced adown a forest-aisle
   And taught me from the store
Of simple airs your lyric lips
   Shall sing for evermore.

In what array your beauty came—
   I sang it as I might;
So sings the pupil blackbird, so
   The poet of the night;

The thrush, a student of your dance,
   Divinely serenades
Your revelation of the limbs
   That twinkle in the glades.

Should I within your leafy school
   The only scholar sit
To pipe discordantly, and be
   Less trusted than the tit?

Not so, sweet country Muse! The wood
   Demands the scanty gown;
Why should their London velvets clog
   Your dances on the down?

I have not shamed you, O my love,
   So friendly and so wild!
You shall not blush to teach again
   Your lover and your child!

III

Who call me base must think me base ;

But soon afresh for me

Your speeding footsteps in the grass

Shall prove my purity !

Printed by T. and A. CONSTABLE, Printers to Her Majesty,
at the Edinburgh University Press.

List of Books

in

Belles Lettres

ALL BOOKS IN THIS CATALOGUE
ARE PUBLISHED AT NET PRICES

1893

Telegraphic Address—
        'BODLEIAN, LONDON'

'A WORD must be said for the manner in which the publishers have produced the volume (*i.e.* "The Earth Fiend"), a sumptuous folio, printed by CONSTABLE, the etchings on Japanese paper by MR. GOULDING. The volume should add not only to MR. STRANG'S fame but to that of MESSRS. ELKIN MATHEWS AND JOHN LANE, who are rapidly gaining distinction for their beautiful editions of belles-lettres.'—*Daily Chronicle*, Sept. 24, 1892.

Referring to MR. LE GALLIENNE'S 'English Poems' *and* 'Silhouettes' by MR. ARTHUR SYMONS :—' We only refer to them now to note a fact which they illustrate, and which we have been observing of late, namely, the recovery to a certain extent of good taste in the matter of printing and binding books. These two books, which are turned out by MESSRS. ELKIN MATHEWS AND JOHN LANE, are models of artistic publishing, and yet they are simplicity itself. The books with their excellent printing and their very simplicity make a harmony which is satisfying to the artistic sense.'—*Sunday Sun*, Oct. 2, 1892.

' MR. LE GALLIENNE is a fortunate young gentleman. I don't know by what legerdemain he and his publishers work, but here, in an age as stony to poetry as the ages of Chatterton and Richard Savage, we find the full edition of his book sold before publication. How is it done, MESSRS. ELKIN MATHEWS AND JOHN LANE? for, without depreciating MR. LE GALLIENNE'S sweetness and charm, I doubt that the marvel would have been wrought under another publisher. These publishers, indeed, produce books so delightfully that it must give an added pleasure to the hoarding of first editions.'—KATHARINE TYNAN in *The Irish Daily Independent*.

' To MESSRS. ELKIN MATHEWS AND JOHN LANE almost more tha to any other, we take it, are the thanks of the grateful singer especially due ; for it is they who have managed, by means of limited editions and charming workmanship, to impress book-buyers with the belief that a volume may have an æsthetic and commercial value. They have made it possible to speculate in the latest discovered poet, as in a new company—with the difference that an operation in the former can be done with three half-crowns.'
St James's Gazette.

List of Books

IN

BELLES LETTRES

(*Including some Transfers*)

PUBLISHED BY

Elkin Mathews and John Lane

The Bodley Head

VIGO STREET, LONDON, W.

N.B.—The Authors and Publishers reserve the right of reprinting any book in this list if a second edition is called for, except in cases where a stipulation has been made to the contrary, and of printing a separate edition of any of the books for America irrespective of the numbers to which the English editions are limited. The numbers mentioned do not include the copies sent for review or to the public libraries.

ADDLESHAW (PERCY).
  POEMS. 12mo. 5s. net. [*In preparation.*

ALLEN (GRANT).
  THE LOWER SLOPES : A Volume of Verse. 600 copies.
  Fcap. 8vo. 5s. net. [*Immediately.*

ANTÆUS.
  THE BACKSLIDER AND OTHER POEMS. 100 only.
    Small 4to. 7s. 6d. net. [*Very few remain.*

BEECHING (H. C.), J. W. MACKAIL, &
        J. B. B. NICHOLS
  LOVE IN IDLENESS. With Vignette by W. B. SCOTT.
    Fcap. 8vo, half vellum. 12s. net. [*Very few remain.*
    Transferred by the Authors to the present Publishers.

BENSON (ARTHUR CHRISTOPHER).
POEMS. 550 copies. 12mo. 5s. net.

BENSON (EUGENE).
FROM THE ASOLAN HILLS : A Poem. 300 copies. Imp.
16mo. 5s. net.   [*Very few remain.*

BINYON (LAWRENCE).
POEMS. 12mo. 5s. net.   [*In preparation.*

BOURDILLON (F. W.).
A LOST GOD : A Poem. With Illustrations by H. J. FORD.
500 copies. 8vo. 6s. net.   [*Very few remain.*

BOURDILLON (F. W.).
AILES D'ALOUETTE. Poems printed at the private press
of Rev. H. DANIEL, Oxford. 100 only. 16mo.
£1, 10s. net.   [*Very few remain.*

BRIDGES (ROBERT).
THE GROWTH OF LOVE. Printed in Fell's old English
type at the private press of Rev. H. DANIEL, Oxford.
100 only. Fcap. 4to. £2, 12s. 6d. net.
          [*Very few remain.*

COLERIDGE (HON. STEPHEN).
THE SANCTITY OF CONFESSION : A Romance. Second
Edition. Crown 8vo. 3s. net.   [*A few remain.*

CRANE (WALTER).
RENASCENCE: A Book of Verse. Frontispiece and 38
designs by the Author. Imp. 16mo. 7s. 6d. net.
          [*Very few remain.*
Also a few fcap. 4to. £1, 1s. net. And a few fcap. 4to, Japanese
vellum. £1, 15s. net.

CROSSING (WM.).
THE ANCIENT CROSSES OF DARTMOOR. With 11 plates.
8vo, cloth. 4s. 6d. net.   [*Very few remain.*

DAVIDSON (JOHN).

PLAYS: An Unhistorical Pastoral; A Romantic Farce;
Bruce, a Chronicle Play; Smith, a Tragic Farce;
Scaramouch in Naxos, a Pantomime, with a Frontis-
piece, Title-page, and Cover Design by AUBREY
BEARDSLEY. 500 copies. Small 4to. 7s. 6d. net.
[*Immediately.*

DAVIDSON (JOHN).

FLEET STREET ECLOGUES. Second Edition. Fcap. 8vo,
buckram. 5s. net.

DAVIDSON (JOHN).

A RANDOM ITINERARY: Prose Sketches. With a Ballad.
Fcap. 8vo. Uniform with 'Fleet Street Eclogues.' 5s. net.
[*Immediately.*

DAVIDSON (JOHN).

THE NORTH WALL. Fcap. 8vo. 2s. 6d. net.
*The few remaining copies transferred by the Author
to the present Publishers.*

DE GRUCHY (AUGUSTA).

UNDER THE HAWTHORN, AND OTHER VERSES. Frontispiece by WALTER CRANE. 300 copies. Crown 8vo.
5s. net. [*Very few remain.*
Also 30 copies on Japanese vellum. 15s. net.

DE TABLEY (LORD).

POEMS, DRAMATIC AND LYRICAL. By JOHN LEICESTER
WARREN (Lord De Tabley). Illustrations and Cover
Design by C. S. RICKETTS. Second Edition.
Crown 8vo. 7s. 6d. net.

DIAL (THE).

No. 1 of the Second Series. Illustrations by RICKETTS,
SHANNON, PISSARRO. 200 only. 4to. £1, 1s. net.
[*Very few remain.*
The present series will be continued at irregular intervals.

EGERTON (GEORGE).

KEYNOTES : Short Stories.   Crown 8vo.   3s. 6d. net.

FIELD (MICHAEL).

SIGHT AND SONG.   (Poems on Pictures.)   400 copies.
12mo.   5s. net.   [*Very few remain.*

FIELD (MICHAEL).

STEPHANIA : A Trialogue in Three Acts.   250 copies.
Pott 4to.   6s. net.   [*Very few remain.*

GALE (NORMAN).

ORCHARD SONGS.   Fcap. 8vo.   With Title-page and
Cover Design by WILL ROTHENSTEIN.   5s. net.

Also a Special Edition limited in number on small paper (Whatman)
bound in English vellum.   £1, 1s. net.

GARNETT (RICHARD).

A VOLUME OF POEMS.   350 copies.   Crown 8vo.   With
Title-page designed by J. ILLINGWORTH KAY.   5s. net.
                                          [*Immediately.*

GOSSE (EDMUND).

THE LETTERS OF THOMAS LOVELL BEDDOES.   Now
first edited.   Pott 8vo.   5s. net.

                                          [*Immediately.*

GRAHAME (KENNETH).

PAGAN PAPERS : A Volume of Essays.   Fcap. 8vo.
5s. net.   [*Immediately.*

GREENE (G. A.).

ITALIAN LYRISTS OF TO-DAY.   Translations in the
original metres from about thirty-five living Italian
poets, with bibliographical and biographical notes.
Crown 8vo.   5s. net.

HAKE (DR. T. GORDON).
> A Selection from his Poems. Edited by Mrs. Meynell. Crown 8vo. 5s. net. [*Immediately.*

HALLAM (ARTHUR HENRY).
> The Poems, together with his essay 'On Some of the Characteristics of Modern Poetry and on the Lyrical Poems of Alfred Tennyson.' Edited, with an Introduction, by Richard Le Gallienne. 550 copies. Fcap. 8vo. 5s. net. [*Very few remain.*

HAMILTON (COL. IAN).
> The Ballad of Hadji and other Poems. Etched Frontispiece by Wm. Strang. 550 copies. 12mo. 3s. net.
> *Transferred by the Author to the present Publishers.*

HAYES (ALFRED).
> The Vale of Arden and Other Poems. With Title-page and Cover Design by Laurence Housman. Fcap. 8vo. 5s. net. [*In preparation.*

HICKEY (EMILY H.).
> Verse Tales, Lyrics and Translations. 300 copies. Imp. 16mo. 5s. net.

HORNE (HERBERT P.).
> Diversi Colores : Poems. With ornaments by the Author. 250 copies. 16mo. 5s. net.

IMAGE (SELWYN).
> Carols and Poems. With decorations by H. P. Horne. 250 copies. 5s. net. [*In preparation.*

JAMES (W. P.).
> Romantic Professions : A Volume of Essays. Crown 8vo. 5s. net. [*Immediately.*

JOHNSON (EFFIE).
> In the Fire and Other Fancies. Frontispiece by Walter Crane. 500 copies. Imp. 16mo. 3s. 6d. net.

JOHNSON (LIONEL).

THE ART OF THOMAS HARDY: Six Essays. With
Etched Portrait by WM. STRANG, and Bibliography
by JOHN LANE. Crown 8vo. 5s. 6d. net.

Also 150 copies, large paper, with proofs of the portrait. £1, 1s.
net.   [*Very shortly.*

JOHNSON (LIONEL).

A VOLUME OF POEMS. 12mo. 5s. net. [*In preparation.*

KEATS (JOHN).

THREE ESSAYS, now issued in book form for the first time.
Edited by H. BUXTON FORMAN. With Life-mask
by HAYDON. Fcap. 4to. 10s. 6d. net.
[*Very few remain.*

LEATHER (R. K.).

VERSES. 250 copies. Fcap. 8vo. 3s. net.
Transferred by the Author to the present Publishers.

LEATHER (R. K.), & RICHARD LE GALLIENNE.

THE STUDENT AND THE BODY-SNATCHER AND OTHER
TRIFLES. 250 copies. Royal 18mo. 3s. net.
Also 50 copies large paper. 7s. 6d. net.   [*Very few remain.*

LE GALLIENNE (RICHARD).

PROSE FANCIES. With Cover Design and Title-page by
WILL ROTHENSTEIN. 5s. net.
Also a limited large paper edition. 12s. 6d. net. [*In preparation.*

LE GALLIENNE (RICHARD).

THE BOOK BILLS OF NARCISSUS. An Account rendered
by RICHARD LE GALLIENNE. Second Edition.
Crown 8vo, buckram. 3s. 6d. net.

LE GALLIENNE (RICHARD).
ENGLISH POEMS. Second Edition, 12mo. 5s. net.

LE GALLIENNE (RICHARD).
GEORGE MEREDITH: Some Characteristics. With a Biblio-
graphy (much enlarged) by JOHN LANE, portrait, etc.
Third Edition. Crown 8vo. 5s. 6d. net.

LE GALLIENNE (RICHARD).
THE RELIGION OF A LITERARY MAN. Fcap. 8vo.
3s. 6d. net.
Also a special edition on hand-made paper. 10s. 6d. net.
[Immediately.

LETTERS TO LIVING ARTISTS.
500 copies. Fcap. 8vo. 3s. 6d. net. *Very few remain.*

MARSTON (PHILIP BOURKE).
A LAST HARVEST: LYRICS AND SONNETS FROM THE
BOOK OF LIFE. Edited by LOUISE CHANDLER
MOULTON. 500 copies. Post 8vo. 5s. net.
Also 50 copies on large paper, hand-made. 10s. 6d. net.
[Very few remain.

MARTIN (W. WILSEY).
QUATRAINS, LIFE'S MYSTERY AND OTHER POEMS. 16mo.
2s. 6d. net. *[Very few remain.*

MARZIALS (THEO.).
THE GALLERY OF PIGEONS AND OTHER POEMS. Post 8vo.
4s. 6d. net. *[Very few remain*
Transferred by the Author to the present Publishers.

MEYNELL (MRS.), (ALICE C. THOMPSON).
POEMS. Second Edition. Fcap. 8vo. 3s. 6d. net. A
few of the 50 large paper copies (First Edition) remain.
12s. 6d. net.

MEYNELL (MRS.).

THE RHYTHM OF LIFE, AND OTHER ESSAYS. Second Edition. Fcap. 8vo. 3s. 6d. net. A few of the 50 large paper copies (First Edition) remain. 12s. 6d. net.

MURRAY (ALMA).

PORTRAIT AS BEATRICE CENCI. With critical notice containing four letters from ROBERT BROWNING. 8vo, wrapper. 2s. net.

NETTLESHIP (J. T.).

ROBERT BROWNING : Essays and Thoughts. Third Edition. Crown 8vo. 5s. 6d. net. Half a dozen of the Whatman large paper copies (First Edition) remain. £1, 1s. net.

NOBLE (JAS. ASHCROFT).

THE SONNET IN ENGLAND AND OTHER ESSAYS. Title-page and Cover Design by AUSTIN YOUNG. 600 copies. Crown 8vo. 5s. net.

Also 50 copies large paper. 12s. 6d. net.

NOEL (HON. RODEN).

POOR PEOPLE'S CHRISTMAS. 250 copies. 16mo. 1s. net.
[*Very few remain.*

OXFORD CHARACTERS.

A series of lithographed portraits by WILL ROTHENSTEIN, with text by F. YORK POWELL and others. To be issued monthly in term. Each number will contain two portraits. Part I. ready Sept. 1893, will contain portraits of SIR HENRY ACLAND, K.C.B., F.R.S., M.D., and of Mr. W. A. L. FLETCHER, of Christ-church, President of the University Boat Club. 350 copies only, folio, wrapper, 5s. net per part ; 50 special copies containing proof impressions of the portraits signed by the artist, 10s. 6d. net per part.

PINKERTON (PERCY).

GALEAZZO : A Venetian Episode and other Poems. Etched Frontispiece. 16mo. 5s. net.
[*Very few remain.*
Transferred by the Author to the present Publishers.

RADFORD (DOLLIE).
SONGS. A New Volume of Verse.   [*In preparation.*

RADFORD (ERNEST).
CHAMBERS TWAIN. Frontispiece by WALTER CRANE.
250 copies. Imp. 16mo. 5s. net.
Also 50 copies large paper. 10s. 6d. net.   [*Very few remain.*

RHYMERS' CLUB, THE BOOK OF THE.
A second series is in preparation.

SCHAFF (DR. P.).
LITERATURE AND POETRY: Papers on Dante, etc.
Portrait and Plates, 100 copies only. 8vo. 10s. net.

SCOTT (WM. BELL).
A POET'S HARVEST HOME: WITH AN AFTERMATH.
300 copies. 12mo. 5s. net.   [*Very few remain.*
* *Will not be reprinted.*

STODDARD (R. H.).
THE LION'S CUB; WITH OTHER VERSE. Portrait.
100 copies only, bound in an illuminated Persian
design. Fcap. 8vo. 5s. net.   [*Very few remain.*

SYMONDS (JOHN ADDINGTON).
IN THE KEY OF BLUE, AND OTHER PROSE ESSAYS.
Cover designed by C. S. RICKETTS. Second Edition.
Thick Crown 8vo. 8s. 6d. net.

THOMPSON (FRANCIS).
A VOLUME OF POEMS. With Frontispiece, Title-page and
Cover Design by LAURENCE HOUSMAN. 500 Copies.
Pott 4to. 5s. net.   [*In preparation.*

TODHUNTER (JOHN).
A SICILIAN IDYLL. Frontispiece by WALTER CRANE.
250 copies. Imp. 16mo. 5s. net.
Also 50 copies large paper, fcap. 4to. 10s. 6d. net.
[*Very few remain.*

TOMSON (GRAHAM R.).

AFTER SUNSET. A Volume of Poems. With Title-page and Cover Design by R. ANNING BELL. 12mo. 5s. net.
Also a limited large paper edition. 12s. 6d. net. [*In preparation.*

TREE (H. BEERBOHM).

THE IMAGINATIVE FACULTY : A Lecture delivered at the Royal Institution. With portrait of Mr. TREE from an unpublished drawing by the Marchioness of Granby. Fcap. 8vo, boards. 2s. 6d. net.

TYNAN HINKSON (KATHARINE).

CUCKOO SONGS. With Title-page and Cover Design by LAURENCE HOUSMAN. 500 copies. 5s. net.
[*In preparation.*

VAN DYKE (HENRY).

THE POETRY OF TENNYSON. Third Edition, enlarged. Crown 8vo. 5s. 6d. net.
The late Laureate himself gave valuable aid in correcting various details.

WATSON (WILLIAM).

THE ELOPING ANGELS : A Caprice. Second Edition. Square 16mo, buckram. 3s. 6d. net.

WATSON (WILLIAM).

EXCURSIONS IN CRITICISM : being some Prose Recreations of a Rhymer. Second Edition. 12mo. 5s. net.

WATSON (WILLIAM).

THE PRINCE'S QUEST, AND OTHER POEMS. With a Bibliographical Note added. Second Edition. 12mo. 4s. 6d. net.

WEDMORE (FREDERICK).

PASTORALS OF FRANCE—RENUNCIATIONS. A volume of Stories. Title-page by JOHN FULLEYLOVE, R.I. Crown 8vo. 5s. net.
A few of the large paper copies of Renunciations (First Edition) remain. 10s. 6d. net.

WICKSTEED (P. H.).
Dante. Six Sermons. Third Edition. Crown 8vo.
2s. net.

WILDE (OSCAR).
The Sphinx. A poem decorated throughout in line and
colour, and bound in a design by Charles Ricketts.
250 copies. £2, 2s. net. 25 copies large paper.
£5, 5s. net. [*In preparation.*

WILDE (OSCAR).
The incomparable and ingenious history of Mr. W. H.,
being the true secret of Shakespear's sonnets now for
the first time here fully set forth, with initial letters
and cover design by Charles Ricketts. 500 copies.
10s. 6d. net. .
Also 50 copies large paper. 21s. net. [*In preparation.*

WILDE (OSCAR).
Dramatic Works, now printed for the first time with a
specially designed Title-page and binding to each
volume, by Charles Shannon. 500 copies. 7s. 6d.
net per vol.
Also 50 copies large paper. 15s. net per vol.
Vol. I. Lady Windermere's Fan : A Comedy in
Four Acts.
Vol. II. A Woman of No Importance : A Comedy
in Four Acts.
Vol. III. The Duchess of Padua : A Blank Verse
Tragedy in Five Acts. [*In preparation.*

WILDE (OSCAR).
Salomé : A Tragedy in one Act, done into English.
With 11 Illustrations, title-page, and Cover Design
by Aubrey Beardsley. 500 copies. 15s. net.
Also 100 copies, large paper. 30s. net. [*In preparation.*

WYNNE (FRANCES).
Whisper. A Volume of Verse. With a Memoir by
Katharine Tynan and a Portrait added. Fcap. 8vo,
buckram. 2s. 6d. net.
Transferred by the Author to the present Publishers.

The Hobby Horse

A new series of this illustrated magazine will be published quarterly by subscription, under the Editorship of Herbert P. Horne. Subscription £1 per annum, post free, for the four numbers. Quarto, printed on hand-made paper, and issued in a limited edition to subscribers only. The Magazine will contain articles upon Literature, Music, Painting, Sculpture, Architecture, and the Decorative Arts; Poems; Essays; Fiction; original Designs; with reproductions of pictures and drawings by the old masters and contemporary artists. There will be a new title-page and ornaments designed by the Editor. Among the contributors to the Hobby Horse are:

The late MATTHEW ARNOLD.
LAWRENCE BINYON.
WILFRID BLUNT.
FORD MADOX BROWN.
The late ARTHUR BURGESS.
E. BURNE-JONES, A.R.A.
AUSTIN DOBSON.
RICHARD GARNETT, LL.D.
A. J. HIPKINS, F.S.A.
SELWYN IMAGE.
LIONEL JOHNSON.
RICHARD LE GALLIENNE.
SIR F. LEIGHTON, Bart., P.R.A.
T. HOPE MCLACHLAN.
MAY MORRIS.
C. HUBERT H. PARRY, Mus. Doc.
A. W. POLLARD.

F. YORK POWELL.
CHRISTINA G. ROSSETTI.
W. M. ROSSETTI.
JOHN RUSKIN, D.C.L., LL.D.
FREDERICK SANDYS.
The late W. BELL SCOTT.
FREDERICK J. SHIELDS.
J. H. SHORTHOUSE.
JAMES SMETHAM.
SIMEON SOLOMON.
A. SOMERVELL.
The late J. ADDINGTON SYMONDS.
KATHARINE TYNAN.
G. F. WATTS, R.A.
FREDERICK WEDMORE.
OSCAR WILDE.
ETC. ETC.

Prospectuses on Application.

THE BODLEY HEAD, VIGO STREET, LONDON, W.

'Nearly every book put out by Messrs. Elkin Mathews &
John Lane, at the Sign of the Bodley Head, is a satisfaction to
the special senses of the modern bookman for bindings, shapes,
types, and papers. They have surpassed themselves, and
registered a real achievement in English bookmaking by the
volume of "Poems, Dramatic and Lyrical," of Lord De Tabley.'
Newcastle Daily Chronicle.

'A ray of hopefulness is stealing again into English poetry
after the twilight greys of Clough and Arnold and Tennyson.
Even unbelief wears braver colours. Despite the jeremiads,
which are the dirges of the elder gods, England is still a nest
of singing-birds (*teste* the Catalogue of Elkin Mathews and John
Lane).'—Mr. ZANGWILL in *Pall Mall Magazine.*